can't
scare
me!

BY ASHLEY BRYAN

too-de-loo-de-loo-de-loo

Atheneum Books for Young Readers
New York · London · Toronto · Sydney · New Delhi

atheneum

ATHENEUM BOOKS FOR YOUNG READERS

An imprint of Simon & Schuster Children's Publishing Division

1230 Avenue of the Americas, New York, New York 10020

Copyright © 2013 by Ashley Bryan

Originally told in *Folk-Lore: Lore of the Antilles, French and English* . . . by Elsie Clews Parson, retold by Ashley Bryan

ATHENEUM BOOKS FOR YOUNG READERS is a registered trademark of Simon & Schuster, Inc.

Atheneum logo is a trademark of Simon & Schuster, Inc.

For information about special discounts for bulk purchases, please contact Simon & Schuster Special Sales at 1-866-506-1949 or business@simonandschuster.com.

The Simon & Schuster Speakers Bureau can bring authors to your live event. For more information or to book an event, contact the Simon & Schuster Speakers Bureau at 1-866-248-3049 or visit our website at www.simonspeakers.com.

The text for this book is set in Grit Primer.

The illustrations for this book are rendered in tempera and watercolor.

Manufactured in China

0613 SCP

First Edition

10 9 8 7 6 5 4 3 2 1

Library of Congress Cataloging-in-Publication Data

Bryan, Ashley.

Can't scare me! / Ashley Bryan. — 1st ed.

p. cm.

Summary: A fearless little boy ignores Grandma's warning about nighttime monsters until he runs away and meets the two-headed giant's three-headed brother.

ISBN 978-1-4424-7657-8

ISBN 978-1-4424-7658-5 (eBook)

[1. Stories in rhyme. 2. Fear—Fiction. 3. Behavior—Fiction. 4. Monsters—Fiction.
5. Grandmothers—Fiction. 6. Blacks—Africa—Fiction.] I. Title. II. Title: Cannot scare me!

PZ8.3.B8286Can 2013

[E]—dc23   2013001490

There once was a boy who knew no fear; he was oh so wild.

He'd scare the lions, stamp his feet—a willful, thrillful child.
He thought he was so big, so tough, though only half past seven,
No one dared to even think of what he'd be like at eleven.

His parents threw their hands up; they knew they needed aid.
That's when they went to Grandma, who told stories in the shade.

Grandma clapped her hands and welcomed in the boy.
She knew that well-told stories were more soothing than a toy.
She told him 'bout a giant; held him close, then told another
Of a two-headed giant and his three-headed brother.

Said, "They wander home at night,
Don't let them ever meet you.
If you're outside after dark,
They'll catch you and they'll eat you."

The little boy laughed.

"Ha! You can't scare me.

I'll escape from any old giant—

one head, two, or three."

Early the next morning, with a basket and a hoe,

They walked to her fields. They began to hoe a row.

The grandson slipped away as soon as he could.

He knew that he shouldn't, but he knew that he would.

He ran back to a mango tree they'd passed along the route.
He climbed among the branches, eating fresh, ripe mango fruit.
He ate up all the mangoes, then he sang and played his flute.

Too-de-loo-de-loo-de-loot!

"Tanto, tanto, I'm wild and I'm free.
Grandma's stories can't scare me.
I'm bold! I'm brave!
And though I may be small,
No many-headed giant
Scares ME at all."

The sun was going down. He had spent a carefree day.
But now he missed his granny and got started on his way.
He skipped along and played his flute.
Too-de-loo-de-loo-de-loot!

He bumped into someone. **Bong!** Brugada-brugada-bop!
It was a great big giant with **two heads** on top.

The giant said, "Oh, little boy, I heard your flute and song.
Keep playing. How I love it! I could listen all day long."

"My granny told me 'bout you," said the boy. "I have no fears
Of two-headed giants and their very many ears.

"Tanto, tanto, I'm wild and I'm free.
Grandma's stories can't scare me.
I'm bold! I'm brave! And though I may be small,
No many-headed giant scares ME at all."

**Giant Two Heads wiggled his four ears.
"They loved your song," he said.**
"Now keep on singing. Run along. My brother's just ahead."

"Good-bye, Two Heads! Farewell, Four Ears!
Your brother's on this route?
Well, I fearlessly welcome giants with my singing and my flute."

Then he bumped into the brother.

Bong!

Brugada-brugada-bop!

Oh, this giant was much bigger

And with **three** heads set on top!

Giant Three Heads said, "Oh, little boy, I heard your flute and song.
Keep playing. How I love it! I could listen all day long!"
The little boy sang and played his flute.
Too-de-loo-de-loo-de-loot!

"Tanto, tanto, I'm wild and I'm free.
Grandma's stories can't scare me.
I'm bold! I'm brave! And though I may be small,
No many-headed giant scares ME at all."

Giant Three Heads laughed out loud, guffawing.
"Ho! Ho! Ho!
I'd like to hear that song again. Hop up on my big toe.
My six ears hear much better
When you come in close.
You say you're not afraid—
Or is that just a boast?"

The boy, to show he had no fear, hopped to the giant's toe.
The seated giant tapped his knee, impatient for the show.

The little boy sang and played his flute.
Too-de-loo-de-loo-de-loot!

"Tanto, tanto, I'm wild and I'm free.
Grandma's stories can't scare me.
I'm bold! I'm brave! And though I may be small,

No many-headed giant
scares ME at all."

The giant laughed.
"You're not afraid, and so you must agree,
Six ears will hear much better
If you hop up on my knee."

The boy hopped to the giant's knee and
Perched there like a bird.
He now was so much closer,
He was sure he would be heard.

He sang his song and played his flute.
Too-de-loo-de-loo-de-loot!

"Tanto, tanto, I'm wild and I'm free.
Grandma's stories can't scare me.
I'm bold! I'm brave! And though I may be small,

**No many-headed giant
Scares ME at all."**

Giant Three Heads rubbed his ears and said, "I am impressed!
You know I'll hear much better if you jump up on my chest."

The boy stood on the giant's thigh, then leaped into the air.
And plopped down on the giant's chest,
To prove he had no fear.

He sang his song and played his flute.
Too-de-loo-de-loo-de-loot!

"Tanto, tanto, I'm wild and I'm free.
Grandma's stories can't scare me.
I'm bold! I'm brave! And though I may be small,
No many-headed giant scares ME at all."

Giant Three Heads flapped six ears and tapped him on the back.
Then snatched him off his burly chest
And threw him in a sack.

Heading home, sack in hand, he sang the poor boy's song.
Sang,

**"TANTA-BARADOO-DALA,
DALALA-BALA-CHA-CHA-CHA!"**

But, oh, he got it wrong!

The giant massacred the song; the scared boy's ears were ringing.
He hoped he'd never hear again such awful off-key singing.

"TANTA-BARANG!"

The giant sang!

His singing voice was horrible, a rumbling in the air.
It terrified the little boy.

AHA! He NOW knew FEAR!

too-de-loo-de-loo-de-loo-de-loo-de-loo

Once home, the giant cried to Jane, who was his household cook.
"I've brought a boy to fatten up. I've bagged him, Janey, look!"
She took the boy out from the sack and bid him play and sing.
Then put him back and closed the sack and tied it with a string.

Next day he said to Janey, as she cleared his breakfast plate,

"I think I'll eat the boy tonight. I just can't wait.

Instead of getting fatter,

He might be getting thinner.

So cook him up for me tonight,

I'll eat the lad for dinner."

The giant left. Then Janey said, "Before I baste and broil you,
Please play for me your song again,
I'm sure that THAT won't spoil you."

"Open the bag a teeny bit, fresh air will clear my flute.
I'll play and sing, you'll dance and swing to
Too-de-loo-de-loo-de-loot."

Janey opened the bag a bit to free his arms and head.
He sang his song and played his flute.
Too-de-loo-de-loo-de-loot!

Janey swung, she swayed, she swirled, she stamped the final beat.
"Encore! Encore!"
She cried for more. "Your music thrills my feet."

"Open the bag a wee bit more, till it's around my middle.
You'll dance upon the tip of your toes, with tippity-tappity-tiddle."

"Oh, tippity-tappity-tiddle!"
Cried Jane.
And she was very sure
That if she tied him farther down,
He'd still be quite secure.

He sang his song and played his flute.
Too-de-loo-de-loo-de-loot!

"Tanto, tanto, I'm wild and I'm free.
Grandma's stories can't scare me.
I'm bold! I'm brave! And though I may be small,
No many-headed giant
Scares ME at all."

Janey tip-tap-toed till dizzy, and still she tapped and spun.
So when the boy stopped playing, she cried,
"What? You've just begun!"

"Open the bag and let me out; you'll never go to bed!
My song will make you turn and twirl.
You'll dance upon your head."

He sang his song and played his flute.
Too-de-loo-de-loo-de-loot!

She shook him out. He looked about.
Jane danced upon her crown,
Then he ran quickly out the door
And left her upside down.

"Come back, come back!" Cook Janey cried.
She twirled back to her feet.
"If you keep running on like that,
You won't be fit to eat."

Faster, faster on he ran, he knew he had no choice.
And even worse than being cooked,
He feared the giant's singing voice!

He ran. He ran. He ran.
He ran past forest, fields, and farms.
He reached his home and dashed indoors,
Right into Grandma's arms.

She didn't push him off or scold.
She hugged him and she kissed him.
She didn't ask him where he'd been,
Just simply said she missed him.

He told her of his close escape,
How Three Heads planned to cheat him,
But that his singing voice was worse
Than any threat to eat him.
How Grandma laughed! He sang his song
While Grandma played his flute.

Too-de-loo-de-loo-de-loot!

"Tanto, tanto, I'm wild and I'm free.
Grandma's stories now teach me
To be bold and brave, though I may be small,
And many-headed giants will scare us all.

"Dear Grandma, now that I know FEAR,
I will be good, don't worry.
If only you would tell me soon . . .

**FOUR-HEADED GIANT'S
STORY!"**